Mollie Evelyn M. Davis

**A Christmas Masque of Saint Roch**

Père Dagobert, and Throwing the wanga

Mollie Evelyn M. Davis

**A Christmas Masque of Saint Roch**
*Père Dagobert, and Throwing the wanga*

ISBN/EAN: 9783337380816

Printed in Europe, USA, Canada, Australia, Japan

Cover: Foto ©Andreas Hilbeck / pixelio.de

More available books at **www.hansebooks.com**

# A Christmas Masque of Saint Roch

## Père Dagobert

and

## Throwing the Wanga

BY

M. E. M. DAVIS

Author of "Under the Man-Fig," "In War Times," "At La
Rose Blanche," "Minding the Gap," Etc.

CHICAGO
A. C. McCLURG AND COMPANY
1896

# CONTENTS.

# A CHRISTMAS MASQUE OF SAINT ROCH.

ST. ROCH'S CHAPEL.

# A CHRISTMAS MASQUE OF ST. ROCH.*

*A small Gothic Chapel set in the midst of a burying ground, on the outskirts of a city.*

## I.

### AT DAWN.

*The Bell, from an ivied niche beneath the surmounting cross of the façade:*

Christ is born, is born!
And o'er the teeming City yonder, lo
A star—the foretorch of the slumbering sun—
Shines palely bright! And guided by its rays,
A thousand little feet go pattering, bare
And white across the floors. And mother-eyes
A-watch, brim o'er with happy tears
Because The Child at Bethlehem is born!

---

*See "Notes," page 57.

9

*Chorus of Dead People:*

But we, with stone and sod upon our breasts?
But we, sealed in these narrow niches? We,
Shut in these stately vaults?—

*Semi-Chorus of Dead Children:*

Our baby-feet
Are wrapped in cere-cloths, so we cannot walk!

*Semi-Chorus of Dead People:*

Our eyes beneath our coffin-lids are dry!
We have forgot the happy tears we shed
(Or ere we died) because The Child was born!

*Chorus:*

Ah we, with these great stones upon our breasts!
   *The effigy of St. Roch above the altar in the Chapel.*
      Christ is born, is born!
(*Dreamily*) I mind me of the skies in Languedoc.
How blue they were at Noël-tide! And I—
A little lad marked by His cross from birth—

(But heeding naught of that!) so danced and
    sang
Along those old Montpelian streets. that maids
With golden hair came out to see!
                        And then,
The Gift upon me came, by God, His grace.
And I did heal men of the plague.
                        So sirs,
By God, His grace, the painters painted me
Upon their church-walls — Guido, and Rubens,
And Titian; so, on window-panes in gold
And red I stand, and with me my good dog!
—Nay, God have mercy lest I praise myself!
Lord, heal the sick and ease the broken heart!

## II.

### MID-MORN.      AT THE GATE.

*Alphonse, the sexton, a grey-bearded man, sits on a rude bench by the gateway. A small table before him is heaped with tallow-candles and tin candle-sticks. Many people entering and passing on to the Chapel. Beggars and children crowded about the entrance.*

*The Sexton, to himself:*

Christ's mercy, what a sunny day! My willow-trees rejoice as if 'twere spring. Candles, M'sieu? (*to a cynic who pauses at the gate.*)

*Cynic:*

Candles! What should I do with candles!

*Sexton:*

I beg your pardon, M'sieu; I thought—St. Roch—

*Cynic:*

'Tis not your business, man, to think. Stick
to your trade of turning people under ground;
and let your wooden Saint in yonder Chapel
mind his—of getting husbands for a pack of
silly girls to flatter, to deceive, aye, and to wring
their hearts—if such lack-witted, blubbering
slaves dwell in their vapid breasts! (*he passes
within the gateway.*)

*A mother with two children, one a cripple in
her arms:*

Give me some candles, sexton, quick. They
should have burned an inch or more ere now!

*Sexton:*

How many, Madame?

*The Mother:*

My little Lame-foot here is six years old
today. A Christmas-gift he was to us! So,
six small flames about the altar's base shall
burn for him.

13

### The Cripple:

And when they've burned, dear mother, will I walk?

### The Mother:

Yes, truly, if we pray aright, my child.

### The Other Child:

Oh, let us hurry on to pray! I long to see my brother run. Then he can catch the butterflies which tease me so, and flutter high above my reach. (*They pass on.*)

### A Blind Man, led:

I'll burn no candles for the Saint this day! If he can't cure me for the one I gave last year, why let him beat his dog, I say, and send him forth to beg. He'll never cheat me of another cent. (*He passes on.*)

### A Child, shouting:

Sand! Sand! Here's your nice white sand to strew upon your graves! Who'll buy fresh sand?

*A Beggar-woman, to passers-by, whining:*

Charité! Charité, s'il vous plait!

*A One-legged Negro Man, to passers-by, in a wheedling voice:*

I knows my pretty young Mistiss is gwine ter give me a nickel! . I knows my fine young genterman is gwine ter give dis po' ole nigger a dime! . Fo' de Lawd, Marse, I'se got sebenteen chillen an' gran' chillen at home, wi' dey mouf sot fer Chrismus dinner!

*Denise Durand, a Young Girl:*

Yes, give me ten candles. Alphonse. (*She passes on, murmuring:*) Five candles for myself —that I may win him back again: and five for him—that he may suffer none, nor know no ill of any kind. . No, eight for him, and two for me. . Nay, all for him! So he may walk in sunshine, though I brave the storm!

*A Ragged Little Girl, gazing after her:*

My! Ain't she sweet! I'm her!

*Second Ragged Little Girl, who carries a baby sister in her arms:*

*Mais non!* Since one year, me, I 'ave choose Ma'mselle Denise. She's me!

*First Ragged Little Girl:*

You sha'n't have her! She's me!

*Second Ragged Little Girl:*

*Mais non!* I'm 'er! I'm 'er!

*A Man with a child's coffin in his arms:*

Where shall I put this little scrap? It barely lived to draw one breath. 'Tis not much matter where it lies.

*Sexton; they speak in French:*

Nay, lad, the veriest sparrow hath a value in His eyes! Yonder, in the clover-bed, in shadow of a flying buttress of the Chapel, where the wind is never rough,—go dig a nest there for the little thing. Perchance some mother buried near may hear it if it wake and cry at night, and so will rise and comfort it. (*The man passes on.*)

### Gordon Leslie, a Young Man:

Is this the chapel called St. Roch? where folks are wont to come to pray?

### Sexton:

Yes, M'sieu.

### Leslie:

Ah — oh — 'tis a custom here, I'm told, to burn some candles when one prays for — for what one wants?

### Sexton:

*Mais certainement*, M'sieu. If M'sieu will pass at the Chapel, he will see those candle burning now. But, on St. Joseph's day, or on Good Friday, thass the time! *Ciel!* how the eye is dazzle' with those candle on St. Joseph's day!

### Leslie:

Ah, I'll take some candles then, for custom's sake.

*Sexton:*

How many, M'sieu ?

*Leslie:*

Fifty (*the sexton stares*). Oh, I meant twenty-five (*hurriedly reddening*). Give me the usual number. (*The sexton gives him three candles in flat candle-sticks. He holds these awkwardly as he passes on.*)

*A Sewing Woman, very shabbily dressed:*

Two candles, sexton, if you please. (*She passes on.*)

*Beggar-woman follows her whining:*

Charité, Madame, Charité !

*A Ragged Lad:*

I don't want no candles, Mister. I'm goin' to set a minit on one o' them tombstones yonder. (*He passes on.*)

### Child, shouting:

Sand! Sand! Here's your nice sand to sprinkle on your graves! Your nice fresh sand!

### A Man with a spade on his shoulder, sullenly:

I s'pose I've got to dig the grave. It's hard a man can't spend his Christmas Day in peace. Why must the woman, devil take her! die on Christmas eve? (*He passes on.*)

### Sexton, solus:

Poor soul, to die on Christmas eve when all the world is joyous and alive! Here's my last candle. It shall burn for her that she may rest in peace.

## III.

### NOON. WITHIN THE CHAPEL.

*Many candles burning about the foot of the altar. The wooden effigy of St. Roch and his dog above. People kneeling. The walls are hung with votive offerings.*

*Denise Durand, after her prayer, watching her candles:*

Now, if the third candle from the end — the one that flares and flames as if an unseen spirit blew upon it — if that candle should burn out soonest, then I'll take it for a sign he did not mean the cruel things he said. But if the fifth one soonest sinks, why then I'll know he does not love me any more!

*The Sewing Woman, after her prayer, watching her candles:*

How fast they burn! And yet, before the flames into the sockets sink and die, all will be ended for the child and me. One leap into the River, one cry from those dear baby-lips when over us close the turbid yellow waves, and then—no more fierce longings for the past, no shrinking from the future, no hunger more, nor cold, nor hard-eyed scorn for me or my child.

*The Blind Man:*

A cheating saint, a greedy glutton saint! He'll never make me see, no not unless I burn a dozen candles to his wooden nose. But I'll not, that's flat.

*Leslie, putting down his candles:*

If those fellows at the Club could see me now! Well, let them laugh, I care not, I . . . . . . The good saint, wooden as he looks, knows what *I* want. I'll leave my candles and my wishes in his care. (*He goes out.*)

*The Mother, after her prayer, watching her crippled child:*

I think he's paler than he was! My little

braveling. art thou cold? Lean close to mother, little one. and make thy prayer. thyself, to Jesus that He may heal thee on thy birthday, and on His. . . *Oh God. my boy! my boy! he's dead! Help! Help!*

*The Other Child. frightened:*

And can my brother run?

*The Mother. wildly:*

Oh. he has wings now, he can fly! Oh God, my child!

*Child Outside shouting:*

Sand! here's your nice clean sand to strew upon your graves!

# IV.

*In the burying-ground by the chapel: many tombs about; a few people walking among the graves. A Sun Dial near the main footway.*

*The Cynic, reading the inscription on the dial:*

"I number but the shining hours." Well. precious little work you've got to do, you hoary, moss-grown dial, that's all I have to say. The shining hours in this world are as scarce as honesty in man, or truth and chastity in woman. Yet once I also thought — pshaw, no matter what I thought! (*Sits down on a flat tombstone near the dial.*)

*Leslie comes out of the chapel and leans on the dial.*

*Leslie:*

"I number but the shining hours." Ah, those were shining hours indeed. when — Lord, what a fool a man can be!

23

*Cynic:*

A very just observation indeed, my friend. But add, if men are fools, women in truth are worse than knaves, and so —

*Leslie, angrily:*

Sir, by what right — ?

*Denise, who has approached unperceived, from the chapel:*

Why, Gordon — Mr. Leslie!

*Leslie:*

Denise — Miss Durand! You here?

*Denise, smiling a little:*

Mr. Leslie — you here?

*Leslie:*

Denise, forgive me! When I twitted you about your superstitions — your leaden Virgins and your small St. Josephs standing on their heads and — well — your wonderful St. Roch

24

upon his altar here ; and these same twittings led us on from sneer to counter-sneer, until we quarreled —

*Denise, interrupting :*

Then, you'll admit now — ?

*Leslie, dubiously :*

Oh, as to that —

*Cynic, under his breath :*

Soho! the smothered fire breaks out again. Fools! Well let it scorch them both, aye shrivel them to cinders!

*Denise :*

Nay, Gordon let it pass. I will believe for both of us. But (*curiously*) what are you doing here?

*Leslie, sheepishly :*

To tell the truth Denise, I've got three candles by the altar, there, alight—and all for you—that I might win you back again.

25

*Denise with rapture:*

Oh Gordon! And I have ten alight—and all for you.

*Leslie, tenderly:*

Spendthrift!

*Beggar-woman, approaching:*

Charité, M'sieu! Charité, Ma'mselle! Merci, M'sieu et Madame la Mariée! (*She goes away rattling Gordon's alms in a tin box.*)

*Gordon, looking after her:*

A prophetess, Denise, a prophetess!

*The Sewing Woman comes out of the chapel walking hurriedly. The Cynic springing to his feet at sight of her:*

Margaret!

*Sewing Woman:*

Philip!

*Philip, sneeringly, reseating himself:*

I find you somewhat shabby, Madam, considering—

*Margaret, interrupting fiercely:*

Considering that night and day I drive the
needle to ward off starvation from my child —
and yours!

*Philip:*

Ha, Colburn's money then is spent. Or stay,
the story's old and threadbare, Madam, but 'tis
short — and true. Will you hear it? The
friend, we'll say, beguiles his friend's wife
from her home; then, wearying of her, casts
her off. That's all. Oh, shame on him—a
friend; on you —a wife!

*Margaret, bewildered:*

Colburn . . beguiles? Philip, what
do you mean?

*Philip:*

God! She dares to ask me what I mean!
My home left desolate . . . the man I
trusted my wife and child .

*Margaret, passionately:*

*Who* left it desolate, your home and mine?
Did I not wait there long and weary months

for your return ? For you, who left me to be gone a single day! No word to tell me why you had abandoned wife and child; no tidings save one cruel line to say that we were henceforth naught to you—your wife and child! And then I traced you step by step until I found you here, where for many weary months —too proud to beg your charity—I have fought hunger and despair—not for my own sake, but our child's.

*Philip, trembling:*

But the letter which you wrote    .   .   .
which said that you and Colburn—

*Margaret, turning coldly away:*

I know nothing of such a letter: nor have I seen George Colburn since he left the house with you. The letters I *have* written you have come back to me—unopened. Oh shame on you, Philip, shame on the father of my child!

*Leslie, interposing courteously:*

I beg your pardon sir. Do you speak of George Colburn of *The Cedars.* George Colburn, who exposed the other day that villain and arch traitor, Allan Carr? I chance to know —

*Philip, suddenly enlightened:*

Allan Carr! why I remember now 't was he who brought me news of Margaret's flight with Colburn — and her letter. He who . . . . God forgive me for a dupe, a fool, a brute, an idiot! Margaret —!

*Margaret, upon his breast sobbing:*

Oh, Philip!

*The Sexton comes out of the chapel with the dead body of the little cripple in his arms. The mother follows, mute and anguished.*

*The Other Child, querulously:*

But why does not my brother fly if he has wings? You said he had wings, Mother. If I had wings I'd fly to the top of yonder willow tree. (*They pass on to the gate.*)

*The Blind Man comes out of the chapel. Leslie and Philip drop some coins into his hat.*

### *The Blind Man:*

Lord bless you, gentlemen! I'd liefer hear the silver tinkling in my hat, and feel the smooth round quarters twixt my thumb and finger, any day, than see! Now fetch me home, boy. (*He passes on to the gate.*)

*The Ragged Lad, jumping up with a half-sob from the ground where he has been lying:*

I wisht I hadn't run away from home. 'Taint no fun, nohow. I'm goin' back. I w—want to see my m—mother! (*He passes on to the gate.*)

### *Child, shouting:*

Here's your fresh sand! Here's your last chance to buy some nice fresh sand!

*One-legged Negro, in the distance, shouting lustily:*

I'm gwine home ter give dem sebenteen chillen an' gran'chillen dey Chris'mus tu'key!

*Ragged Little Girl in the distance, crooning to her baby-sister:*

> "Fais dodo, Minette!
> Trois p'ti cochons de lait
> Endormez-moi cette enfant
> Jusqu' à l'age de quinze ans!
> Quand quinze ans sera sonné,
> Nous irons la marier
> Avec joli 'ti Tintin,
> P'ti fils de not' voisin.
> > Fais dodo, Minette
> > Do — do."

*Margaret:*

Come, Philip, let us hasten to our child. (*They pass on, arm in arm, to the gate.*)

*Denise, reading the inscription on the dial:*

"I number but the shining hours." Nay, Gordon, all the hours are shining! (*They pass on, arm in arm, to the gate.*)

## V.

### NIGHT.

*The Bell, from its ivied niche:*

Christ is born, is born!
A yellow rim—the afterglow of day—
Belts in the earth, as if a token-ring
Of God were slipped about it for a sign
Of peace and love.   So belted, blesséd Earth,
Move on among the spheres, and add thy note
Of joy to theirs because The Child is born!

*Chorus of Dead People:*

Sweet is our rest beneath the grassy sod!
Secure our niches in the arching vaults,
Where Pain nor Sorrow may pursue us more.

*Semi-chorus of Dead Children:*

We do not care to walk.   Our little feet
Are safe from all the thorny ways of life.

32

# A CHRISTMAS MASQUE OF ST. ROCH.

*The Baby in the grave by the Chapel:*

But I'm afeard!

*The Woman who died on Christmas Eve:*

Is that a baby's voice?
Mine arms do yearn for one I left behind!
—I'm coming, little one; be not afraid!

*Chorus:*

"'Tis sweet to rest for aye beneath the stones!

*The effigy of St. Roch in the Chapel:*

Christ is born, is born!
(*Dreamily*).   How soft the stars that shone on
   Languedoc!
        .   .        And so those bold Venetians stole
   my bones
And from Montpelier, in a time of plague,
Bore them away to Venice by the sea.
And Doge and Senate welcomed them in state:
And Tintoretto at San Rocco there,

Did paint such wonders that the world stood
   still,
And all for me, who healed him of the plague!
—Nay, God forgive me! If I boast, forgive,
For Thou alone hast power to heal, and Thou
To ease the wounded heart; that so the world
  be blest!

   *A whisper from above that thrills the air:*
   The world be blest!

# PÈRE DAGOBERT.

# PÈRE DAGOBERT.*

None of your meagre, fasting, wild-eyed, spare
Old friars was Father Dagobert!
He paced the streets of the *Vieux Carré*
In seventeen hundred and somewhat, gay,
Rubicund, jovial, round and fat.
He wore a worldly three-cornered hat
On his shaven pate; he had silken hose
To his ample legs; and he tickled his nose
With snuff from a gold *tabatière*.
He listened with courtly, high-bred air
To the soft-eyed *pénitente* who came—
Kirtled lassie, or powdered dame—
To kneel by the carved confessional
And breathe in a whisper musical
The deadliest sin she could recall.

*See "Notes," page 58.

# PÈRE DAGOBERT.

La Nouvelle Orléans' self was young,
When the Père came over from France, a strong,
Handsome, rollicking Capuchin brother,
Poor as a mouse of the Church, his mother,
With a voice like an angel's, sweet and clear,
That saints and sinners rejoiced to hear.
The town it had grown apace, and he
For the goodly half of a century
Had blessed its brides when the banns were said,
And christened its babies and buried its dead;
He had sipped the wines from its finest stores
As he played at chess with its Governors;
And wherever a feast was forward, there
Was a cover for Father Dagobert.

In the midst of its fields of indigo
Where the sleek, black negroes, row on row,
Dug and delved for the brotherhood,
The stately house of the Order stood;
And here at ease on their fine estate
The Père and his Capuchins slept and ate,
And thrived and fattened for many a year,
Ungrudged by none of their royal cheer.

# PÈRE DAGOBERT.

## II.

But over the wall of this paradise
One day the inquisitorial eyes
Of the Spanish Padre Cirilo
Gazed, horror-stricken!
    " Your Grace must know,"
He wrote with haste to the Order's head,
"What shame by our Order here is spread;
An idle, battening set, they dwell—
Unmindful each of his cord and cell—
In a galleried convent, tall and fair,
Misgoverned by one named Dagobert
(A bibulous Frenchman, gross and fat,
Who wears a graceless three-cornered hat,
And takes his snuff from a jeweled box).
They have cunningly carven singing clocks
In their refectory; when they dine
They drink the best and the beadiest wine;
They have silver spoons and forks—nay, more,

They have special spoons for the *café noir*
That clears their brains when the feast is o'er.


"This Dagobert " (so the Padre said)
Usurps the power of the Church's Head.
And cares not a fig what Rome has wrought!
The Santa Cruzada itself is naught:
And thirty years it hath been, in full,
Since Papal or Apostolic Bull
Hath reached his flock; but the people fare
Content to follow the singing Père:
For in truth he sings, and sings, alas!
With a seraph's tongue at the daily mass."


Further he told how this singing priest
Forgot the fast and shifted the feast
Of the Holy Church at his own good will,
With the people blindly following still.
He hinted at comely quadroons a-stare
With bold black eyes at morning prayer
In the convent chapel, or strolling, gay,
Through the convent halls at close of day.

"And the rascals grow daily richer!  Your
   Grace"
(He groaned)  "Must look to this godless
   place,
And humble the head of this haughty friar!"

His Grace was shocked.  With a holy ire
He sped his edict across the sea.
But a wrathful Province heard the decree,
And Governer, Alcalde, citizen staid,
Riffraff, soldier, matron and maid,
All swore nor Church, nor State should dare
To rob them of Father Dagobert!
So back to Spain the Padre went.
Humbled himself, and penitent.
The Père, unruffled, pursued his way,
Disturbed nor vexed to his dying day;
And the friars rejoiced to their convent's core,
And slept and ate at their ease once more.

## III.

Down in the weed-grown Cimetière
St. Louis reposes the worthy Père;
And they say, when the nights are warm and
  sweet,
And stayed is the sound of passing feet,
That he clambers down from his snug retreat
In the crumbling vault, and up and down
The narrow walks, in his fine serge gown
And three-cornered hat, he makes his way,
And sings as he goes, till the break of day;
And the powdered dames of the old *régime*,
And the pig-tail courtiers, all agleam
With jewels and orders, come thronging out
From tombs and vaults—a shadowy rout—
To sit a-top of the mouldy stones
That cover the common plebeian bones,
And listen, all wrapped in a vapory mist;
While the hands they have pressed, the lips
  they have kissed

# PÈRE DAGOBERT.

In the olden days, grow warm again,
And the eyes whereon rusty coins have lain
For a hundred years and more, grow bright
With the deathless joys of a long-gone night.


—A bell in Don Almonaster's tower
By the old Place d'Armes rings out the hour.
Short in his canticle stops the Père
To cross himself and mutter a prayer;
Then he climbs to his chilly resting-place
And pulls his cope up over his face,
And folds his hands in a patient way,
And rests himself through the livelong day.


The dames and courtiers slowly rise,
Brushing the dews from their softened eyes,
And courtesying grandly as they go,
They pass along in a stately row;
They pause at the door of their family tombs—
Glancing askance at the inner glooms,
And lifting a finger with slow demur—
To say with that air of a *connoisseur*

That greeted a Manon, when she and they
Trod the stage of the *vieux carré*,
" *Ma foi!* 'tis a wondrous thing and rare,
The singing of Father Dagobert!"

# THROWING THE WANGA.

# THROWING THE WANGA.*

## ST. JOHN'S EVE.

*Shrill over dark blue Pontchartrain*
*It comes and goes, the weird refrain,*
*Wanga! wanga!*

*The trackless swamp is quick with cries*
*Of noisome things that dip and rise*
*On night-grown wings; and in the deep,*
*Dark pools the monstrous forms that sleep*
*Inert by day uplift their heads.*
*The zela flower its poison sheds*
*Upon the warm and languorous air;*
*The lak-vine weaves its noxious snare;*
*The wide palmetto leaves are stirred*
*By venomed breathings, faintly heard*
*Across the still, star-lighted night.*

---

*See "Notes," page 58.

# THROWING THE WANGA.

*Her lonely spice-fed fire, alight*
*Upon the black swamp's utmost rim,*
*Now spreads and flares, now smoulders dim;*
*And at her feet they curl and break,*
*The dark blue waters of the lake.*

*Her arms are wild above her head—*
*Old withered arms, whose charm has fled.*

    " Zizi, Creole Zizi,
You is slim an' straight ez a saplin'
   Dat grows by de bayou's aidge ;
You is brown an' sleek ez a young Bob White
   Whar hides in de yaller sedge.

"Yo' eyes is black an' shiny,
   An' quick ez de lightnin' flash ;
You wuz bawn in de time er freedom,
   An' never is felt de lash.
     —Me, I kin th'ow wanga ! "

*Her dusky face is wracked and seamed,*
*That once like ebon marble gleamed.*

# THROWING THE WANGA.

Zizi, Creole Zizi,
" You is spry on yo' foot ez de jay-bird
  Whar totes de debble his san';
You kin tole de buckra to yo' side
  By de turnin' o' yo' han'.


"Yo' ways is sweet ez de sugar
  You puts in yo' *pralines*.
When de orange flower on de banquette
  draps,
  An' de pistache-nut is green.
      Me, I kin th'ow wanga!"


*Her knotted shoulders, brown and bare,*
*The deathless scars of slavehood wear.*


  "Zizi, Creole Zizi,
You is crope lak a thieft to de do'-yard
  When de moon wuz shinin' high,
An' you stole de ole man' heart erway
  Wid de laughin' in yo' eye.

" My ole man!—de chillun's daddy!—
  We is hoed de cotton row
An' shucked de corn-shuck side by side
  Fer forty year an' mo'!
    —Me, I kin th'ow wanga!"

*The flames that leap about her feet*
*Burn with a perfume strange and sweet.*

    " Zizi, Creole Zizi,
'Twis' yo'se'f in de coonjine
  Lak a moccasin in the slime;
'Twis' yo'se'f when de fiddle talks
  Fer de las' endurin' time.

Den was'e ter de bone in de midnight,
  In de mawnin' wa'se erway;
Bu'n wid heat in de winter-time,
  An' shiver de hottes' day—
    Wanga! Wanga!

"Onder yo' fla'ntin' *tignon*
  De red-hot beetles crawl,
Wid claws dat sco'ch inter de meat
  An' mek de blood draps fall!

"Over yo' bed de screech-owl
    In de midnight screech an' cry!
Den kiver yo' head, Creole Zizi—
    Den kiver yo' head an' die—
        Wanga! Wanga!"

*Her voice is hushed, she crouches low*
*Above the embers' flickering glow.*
*The swamp-wind wakes, and many a thing*
*Unnamed flits by on furry wing;*
*They brush her cheeks unfelt; she hears*
*The far-off songs of other years.*

*Her eyes grow tender as she sways*
*And croons above the dying blaze.*

"Oh, de cabin at de quarter in de old planta-
        tion days,
    Wid de garden patch behin' it an' de gode-
        vine by de do'.
An' de do'-yard sot wid roses, whar de chil-
        lun runs and plays,
    An' de streak o' sunshine, yaller lak, er-
        slantin' on de flo'!

51

"We wuz young an' lakly niggers when de ole
   man fotch me home.
   Ole Mis' she gin de weddin', an' young
    Mis' she dress de bride!
He say he gwineter love me twel de time o'
   kingdom come,
   An' forty year an' uperds we is trabble side
    by side!

" But ole Mars' wuz killed at Shiloh, an' young
   Mars' at Wilderness:
   Ole Mis' is in de graveyard, wid young
    Mis' by her side.
An' all er we-all's fambly is scattered eas' an'
   wes'.
   An' de gode-vine by de cabin do' an' de
    roses all has died!

" My chillun they is scattered too, an' some is
   onder groun'.
   Hit wuz forty years an' uperds we is trab-
    ble, him an me!

Ole Mis', whar is de glory o' de freedom I
    is foun'?
De ole man he is lef' me fer de young eyes
    o' Zizi! "

*Her arms are wild above her head,*
*The softness from her voice has fled.*

    " Zizi, Creole Zizi,
  'Twis' yo'se'f in de coonjine
Lak a moccasin in de slime;
   Kunjur de ole man wid yo' eye
Fer de las' endurin' time!

" Den cry an' mo'n in de mawnin',
   In de midnight mo'n an' cry,
'Twel de debble has you, han' an' foot,
   Den stretch yo'se'f an' die!—
      Wanga! Wanga!

# NOTES.

# NOTES.

## ST. ROCH.

St. Roch's Chapel : A famous mortuary shrine at New Orleans, much frequented by all classes of people. Candles are burned to ensure answer to prayer.

St. Roch : A mediæval saint born at Montpelier, France (1395). He is said to have come into the world with a small red cross on his breast. Died (1427). His bones were stolen by the Venetians during the plague of 1485, and carried from Montpelier to Venice.

St. Roch is invoked in time of sickness. He is locally invested with extraordinary powers and supposed to be peculiarly potent in obtaining husbands for young women. St. Roch is always represented in company with his dog.

The beautiful church of San Rocco at Venice, decorated by Tintoretto and his pupils, is dedicated to this saint.

Small images of St. Joseph are sold at the

chapel of St. Roch for charms. Vulgar superstition declares that the saint is more efficacious if stood upon his head.

## PÈRE DAGOBERT.

PÈRE DAGOBERT was made Superior of the French Capuchins at New Orleans in 1766. For more than fifty years he continued to be the spiritual father of the Louisiana colonists. The story of his quarrel with Father Cirilo and the Spanish Capuchins is amusingly told by Charles Gayarré in his *History of Louisiana*.

## THROWING THE WANGA.

*To throw the Wanga:* French, *jeter le Wanga:* to cast the Vodoo spell.